JACKSON COUNTY LIBRARY SERVICES
MEDFORD OREGON 97501

D1133869

plus

ices

THE NEW KID

Anne Schraff

SADDLEBACK
EDUCATIONAL PUBLISHING

red rhino
b**OO**ks®

SADDLEBACK
EDUCATIONAL PUBLISHING
www.sdlback.com

Copyright ©2018 by Saddleback Educational Publishing
All rights reserved. No part of this book may be reproduced in any form or by any means, electronic or mechanical, including photocopying, recording, scanning, or by any information storage and retrieval system, without the written permission of the publisher. SADDLEBACK EDUCATIONAL PUBLISHING and any associated logos are trademarks and/or registered trademarks of Saddleback Educational Publishing.

ISBN-13: 978-1-62250-979-9
ISBN-10: 1-62250-979-X
eBook: 978-1-63078-393-8

Printed in Malaysia

22 21 20 19 18   1 2 3 4 5

Paige

Age: 12

Favorite Insect: morpho peleides (blue morpho butterfly)

Hobby: collects My Little Pony figures

Favorite Food: mochi ice cream

Best Quality: supportive

CHARACTERS

Orion

Age: 12 (maybe)

Hometown: "far away"

Hidden Talent: solving unsolvable math problems

Favorite Planet: Kepler 438b

Best Quality: kindness

1
NEW KID

"Coco!" Paige ran up to her friend at school. "I just saw a new kid. He'll be in sixth grade too. He's coming to our classroom."

"Did he seem nice?" Coco asked.

"He was with his mom. I did say hi," Paige said. "You know what? He has green eyes. The color is amazing. I've never seen anything like it. His name is Orion Wells. Funky, huh?"

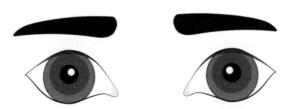

"I hope he's friendly," Coco said. "That's all I care about. Some kids are mean here."

Paige Morgan just turned 12. Coco Lamar had been 12 for a few weeks. The girls had been friends since preschool. Coco was like a sister to Paige. Paige was an only child. Her parents were older than most. They were college professors.

♡ Best ♡
Friends
Forever

"Here he comes," Paige whispered. She gripped Coco's arm.

"Ouch!" Coco said. "You're hurting me, girl."

"I'm sorry," Paige said. "I'm nervous."

"He's just a boy," Coco said, laughing.

"But he's strange," Paige said.

"All boys are strange," Coco said. "My baby brother is strange."

The new boy drew near. "Hi," Coco said. "Welcome to our school! I guess you'll be in our class. I'm Coco. This is Paige."

Orion didn't smile, but he looked nice. His black hair was thick and curly. His skin was tan. "Hello," he said.

"Our teacher is Ms. Nesbit," Coco said. "You'll like her. She's tough but fair." Coco was a much better talker than Paige. She could talk to anyone. Paige was a little shy with strangers.

"Where are you from?" Coco asked. "I heard your name was Orion. Is that right?"

"Yes," the boy said. "I'm from far away."

Coco and Paige looked at each other.

The three kids walked together toward class. Ms. Nesbit hadn't arrived yet. The students sat down.

Orion sat close to Paige. He was on his cell phone. It looked like he was doing math. Coco noticed it too. The girls exchanged another look.

$$F = mg = ma = m \frac{d^2h}{d+2}$$

$$x^2 = A$$

$$x^2 - 3x - 4 = 0$$
$$4x^2 - 3x - 1 = 0$$

$$f(x) = x^2$$

$$\int f(x)dx$$

$f(a)$

a

4

Coco tapped Orion's shoulder. "What are you doing?" she asked.

"It's a math app. Calculus," he said. "Oh, it's so fun."

Coco texted Paige. "What? Is he from outer space? Get real!"

2
THE INSULT

Chills ran up Paige's spine. Outer space?

Ms. Nesbit came into the room then. She was tall and thin. The teacher was pleasant but not pretty. She was very good at her job. The minute she came in, kids put away their phones. The school didn't allow phones in class.

No phones allowed!

"Class," Ms. Nesbit said cheerfully. "Let's welcome our new student. His name is Orion Wells. His family just moved here. We are happy to meet him." The class gave Orion a round of applause. Ms. Nesbit had trained them well. But she was not successful with every student.

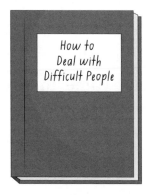

Flynn Morris was a big boy. He didn't do well in class. Flynn was a bully. "What kind of name is Orion? Dude looks like a weirdo," he said softly.

Paige was close enough to hear. What an insult! She didn't think Orion heard it. He was too far away. Still, Orion turned around. He looked right at Flynn.

"Oh man!" Flynn cried out. "I feel sick. My skin's itchy!"

Ms. Nesbit was annoyed. Flynn was always causing problems. "What are you mumbling about, Flynn? Behave yourself."

"The new kid looked at me funny. Now I feel creepy all over. It feels like bugs are crawling on my skin." Flynn was wiggling around at his desk.

9

"Flynn Morris!" Ms. Nesbit snapped. "Stop being silly. Be quiet."

Orion just sat there. He looked down at his books.

It was recess. Paige ran outside. She grabbed Coco. "Did you see what happened this morning?"

"Yeah. Flynn went off about something," Coco said. "But I don't know about what."

"Flynn called Orion a weirdo. I heard it. Orion did too. He must have good ears.

Anyway, Orion turned around. He stared at Flynn." Paige ran out of breath. She was talking fast.

"And what?" Coco asked.

"Orion's eyes glowed. I saw it. It was amazing," Paige said. "He glared at Flynn. Then Flynn felt sick. He said bugs were crawling on him. I never saw anything like it." Paige shook her head. "Did Orion *do* something to him?"

"That's silly," Coco said. "Orion just overheard Flynn. Then he gave him the evil eye. Flynn is a bully and a chicken. He freaked out. The dude can dish it out, for sure. But he can't take it."

"But, Coco," Paige said. "I think Orion has real power. His eyes changed. They glowed! I saw it."

"Come on, Paige. You've been watching

too many scary movies. Orion is just a smart kid. His eyes are green. So what? No big deal. He heard Flynn's nasty slam. Then he stared him down. That's all." Coco sighed. Paige was overreacting. "I'm glad he took Flynn down. He had it coming," she said.

3
ALIENS ON EARTH

That evening Paige did homework. She opened her laptop. Her assignment was on Alexander Hamilton. She was ready to do some work. But she was curious. What about aliens? Were they real?

She typed "aliens on Earth." It was too silly. Of course Orion was human.

Paige read about a man. He lived in England. This man believed he was an alien. "Wow," Paige said aloud to her parents. "Listen to this. Over 20 percent of people believe in ET. They think aliens are real."

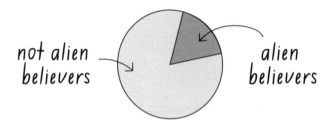

not alien believers   alien believers

Her dad looked up from his work. He was reading student essays. "Well, not me," he said.

"But there *could* be," Paige said. "Right? This says they live as humans. They may be people we know."

Her mom laughed. "I don't think so, honey," she said.

"But people think they've met aliens," Paige said.

Dad pushed his glasses down. Then he looked at his daughter. "This is an odd topic. Why are you so interested? You know UFOs don't exist. There are no aliens."

Paige didn't want to mention Orion. "Oh, I saw this movie ..." she said. Her voice trailed off.

Dad grinned. "I thought so."

Paige didn't say what had happened at school. She continued to read about aliens.

There was another report. It said aliens were here by accident. A spacecraft crashed. There were survivors. They adapted. There was no choice. Nobody should fear them. *"They want to live in peace. It's that simple,"* she read. *"They are more afraid of us."*

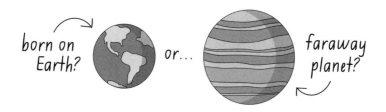

born on Earth? or... faraway planet?

Paige thought about Orion. Maybe that's what happened to him. Maybe his ship crashed. Everyone was lost. Orion and his mom survived. Or maybe he was born on Earth. Paige had so many questions.

She continued to read. *"Let's say you meet someone. They don't seem quite human.*

Don't be afraid. They really are just like us. But some may have special skills."

Paige got goose bumps. What if Orion *was* an alien? And what if he *did* have special skills?

Paige's parents were from England. They came to the US for college. That's where they met.

Often they used British slang. Paige thought it was quirky. Her dad called wackos "nutters." Many people believed silly things. Her dad would laugh. "Those nutters!" he would say. "They are at it again."

where Paige's parents were born   England

Her mom would joke too. "Ah yes! It's a full moon. That always brings out the nutters."

Paige did not want to be a nutter. So she kept quiet.

4

RECESS

It was the next day. The kids were at recess. Orion was sitting alone on a bench. He was eating an apple.

"He looks so lonely," Paige said to Coco. "Let's go over and talk to him."

"Yeah," Coco said. "That's a good idea. Nobody should be alone at recess. I know why you're my friend, Paige. You're a good person."

good person award

BEING A
GOOD PERSON

Paige wasn't sure Orion wanted company. Maybe he was a loner. She was willing to take a chance. Coco had taken a chance on her. Paige never forgot how good it felt.

"Hi, Orion," Coco said. Her smile was wide and friendly. "Is that a good apple? It sure looks yummy."

Orion smiled. He had a nice smile. The boy looked average—except for his eyes. "Yes, it's delicious. I've had apples with no flavor. But this one is perfect."

The Perfect Apple

☑ shiny
☑ crisp
☑ juicy
☑ sweet

"We're going to get apples too. We'll be right back. Come on, Paige," she said.

Soon the girls returned. Orion made room for them. All three sat on the bench. Each had an apple.

"Good apples grow around here," Paige said.

"I like fruit a lot," Orion said. "Better than almost anything else."

"I should eat more fruit," Paige said. "I eat too many sweets."

Orion grinned. "Sweets are okay once in a while."

"Do you like Ms. Nesbit?" Coco asked.

"She seems fine," Orion said. "I always

respect my teachers. That's how I was brought up. We can learn from all kinds of people."

The bell rang then. Recess was over. "Thanks for coming over to talk to me," Orion said. "Not everybody talks to the new kid. You must have kind hearts. I'm glad we're friends."

The girls walked away. "Well, that was good, right?" Paige asked.

Coco laughed. "Totally," she said.

"Still ... I wonder. I feel like he can *see* me. Why?"

22

"What are you talking about?"

"Those eyes! Don't you feel like he knows?" Paige asked. "Like, knows your true self?"

"What? Nobody can do that," Coco said.

"I don't know," Paige said. "There's something off. I like him. He seems like a nice boy. But there's something odd about him. Don't you think? Can't you just feel it? Something sort of spooky."

"Now who's being weird?" Coco said. "Orion is nice and polite. He's not like Flynn. That boy is a bully. When he walks by, kids duck. He snorts like a pig at Koral. Just because she's a little chubby. It's so mean. I saw her crying the other day."

"Does he really do that?" Paige cried. "Oh, that's sick!"

Just then Koral passed by. Flynn was

not far behind. Orion followed. He was a few feet behind the bully. Paige got a weird feeling. Something was about to happen.

Flynn did not see the new boy. Then he started to tease Koral. "*Oink-oink,* little piggy," he sang. "Here, piggy. Get some snacks."

Koral ran. But Flynn chased her.

"Can't run fast, huh? Poor piggy," he teased. The words were cruel.

Suddenly there was a loud noise. Flynn turned. Orion stared at him. His eyes were like emeralds.

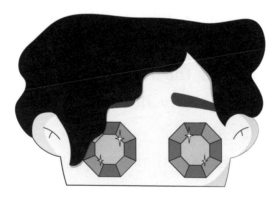

Flynn looked scared. "It's hot!" he screamed. He grabbed his neck. "Aahhh! I'm burning!" He dropped to the grass.

Some students stopped walking.

"What's his deal?" a girl said.

"Flynn's gone loco," another girl said.

"What's up, Flynn?" a boy asked.

"I'm on fire! He … he …" Flynn mumbled. Slowly he got up. Kids were laughing. There was no fire. Things looked normal. Was Flynn nuts?

"Coco," Paige gasped. "Did you see that?"

"Yeah," Coco said softly. "I did."

"Did Orion do that?"

"I don't know," Coco said. "But it was cool!"

5
AN IDEA

It was nighttime. Paige was in bed. Her mind drifted. Was Orion into magic? She had seen magic shows on TV. Magicians seemed to have cool powers. Paige had seen David Copperfield. David Blaine. Criss Angel. She couldn't figure out their tricks. Her dad had said it was fake. Magic was just clever fun.

Alakazam!

Presto chango!

Just then her phone rang. She'd forgotten to turn it off. It was a house rule. No phones at night. Paige had to answer. It was Coco. What did she want? It was probably about the contest.

There was going to be a talent show. It would be in two weeks. Kids from three schools would compete. There would be judges. The winner would get a prize. The prize could be used to buy books. Or go to camp. Or it could be put away for college.

Many gifted kids planned to take part.

This included Coco. She had a beautiful voice. But she did not have self-confidence.

"Hey, Coco," Paige said. "I can't talk long."

"Girl, I wasn't sure you'd answer. I know the rule at your house. But listen. Practice was this afternoon. I heard some other kids. They were *so* good. My song sucks. I want to make my folks proud. But I'm not counting on anything. They have been through hard times. My mom's been sick. Dad was out of work. I want to make them happy."

"You're the best singer in school," Paige said. "I bet you're the best in the state. You could win a TV singing contest!"

"Aw, thanks! I get nervous. Singing in front of people is hard," Coco said. "I'm afraid my voice will crack. Even when I'm singing in church. I look at all those faces. The eyes staring back at me. It's scary."

29

"You'll be great. Pick a song you love. Then it's meant to be. You'll win. That prize is yours," Paige said.

"Girl," Coco said. "Just what I needed to hear. See you tomorrow."

"Later," Paige said, feeling slightly sick. She had held back. Her words were not enough. Coco deserved to win. She *was* great. But Coco's fears were real. The crowds would be large. What if she froze? Paige could praise. She could clap. But Coco could bomb.

Then an idea came to her. She could think of nothing else. Orion! Could he help? He had a gift. Could he cure Coco's fear?

The new boy could stop a bully. It was something in his blazing green eyes. What else could he do?

Paige just had to find out.

6
THE REQUEST

It was lunch. Paige finally got to talk to Orion. He was alone, eating his sandwich. Her heart pounded. "Can I sit here?" she asked.

Orion's sandwich

"This isn't my bench," he said. "I'd love some company." He moved over so she could sit.

"Don't take this the wrong way. I think there's something cool about you. I can't put my finger on it. But you really stopped Flynn cold. All you did was look at him. He's such a mean bully. Your eyes were so bright."

Paige took a breath. Then she kept going. Did she sound silly? Losing her nerve wouldn't be good. She told him about the talent show.

"Well, you know Coco. She's a gifted singer. The contest should be hers. She's nervous, though. The girl's a total chicken. I mean that in the nicest way. Please don't be mad," Paige said.

"But I was thinking. Could you come to the show? I'll save you a seat up front. Maybe you could work some magic. Make Coco brave. You know, with your eyes."

Paige looked down at her hands. What

could Orion be thinking? She couldn't bear to look at him. Would he be mad? She'd discovered his power. Slowly she got the courage to look up.

Orion smiled. Then he laughed. But he said nothing. It was an awkward moment.

"Uh, okay," Paige said. "I understand. See you around." She got up and walked away.

Coco had been in the library. Paige met her as the bell rang. Her friend was excited. She had picked a song for the show. It was called "You Raise Me Up." She knew it was mature. But it was powerful. The song was packed with emotion.

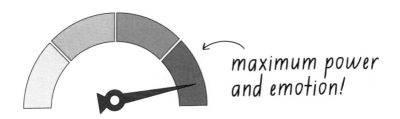

maximum power and emotion!

"It's got heart," Coco said. "I've seen little kids sing it on YouTube. They blew me away. It was amazing. Those judges will like a song like that."

"I like that song too," Paige said. "Brings tears to my eyes."

"Right on, girl," Coco said, laughing.

After school Paige went straight home. She had jazz class that afternoon. Her mom always took her to dance. Paige looked forward to it. Her mom would watch each session. It made Paige feel special.

Mom
the biggest fan

Mother and daughter got into the car. They buckled their seatbelts. "Let's play some Taylor Swift," Paige said. Then she put on the music.

"Mrs. Morris called me today," her mom said. "She was complaining about a new boy. Orion, right? She was pretty mad. Is Orion picking on Flynn? Have you seen anything? She wanted to know."

Paige turned down the volume. "What?" she snorted. "Ugh. Oh no, Mom. Mrs. Morris has it wrong. Flynn is the bully. He bullies everyone. Orion stood up to him."

"Oh, really?" her mom said. "Mrs. Morris thinks Flynn is getting hexed. It's pretty silly. I almost laughed."

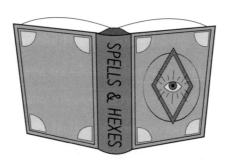

"I can't believe she doesn't know. Flynn is a bad kid," Paige said.

"Nobody wants to think their child is bad. But I guess you're right about him. Your father said something. He plays golf with Tom Norman. Tom's daughter is Koral. She's had a hard time this year. Why didn't you tell me it was so bad?"

"Flynn doesn't bully me. I don't let him," Paige said. "But Koral? She's so sweet.

Flynn teases her all the time. Kids do look out for her. They make sure she's not alone. Well, mostly."

"The family wants to pull her out of school. But you know how people are. I didn't know what to think. You should have said something."

"I'm sorry. It seemed okay. Who knew it got so bad?" Paige said. "Flynn has been nicer. Orion hasn't let him be mean."

"Well," her mom said. "He is not hexing bullies."

Paige stalled. Would her mom believe her? She was dying to tell her. Orion's green eyes had power. They lit up when he was mad. She decided to keep quiet.

7
CONFESSION

As usual Paige and Coco were together. They ate lunch the next day. Orion didn't come. He was at a chess club meeting.

"I'm going to tell you something. Swear you won't get mad," Paige said.

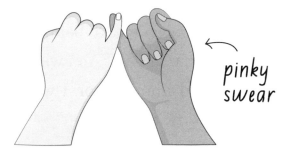

pinky swear

Coco frowned. "What did you do?"

"Ha-ha. It's not about me. I know you

don't believe it. But Orion has special powers. You say his eyes don't light up. Stuff doesn't happen. Bugs didn't attack Flynn. Blah. Blah. Blah," Paige said.

"You're right. I don't believe any of that stuff. The boy just has beautiful eyes. That's all there is to it. Orion tricked Flynn," Coco said firmly. "He made Flynn think he had power. It was real to Flynn."

"Well, I think there's something to it. Orion is magical. He can make bad stuff happen. Maybe he can make good stuff happen too. You've got a beautiful voice. But what if you're afraid? You won't be your best. So I asked him a favor. I want him to sit up front. Work his magic—"

"You did what?!" Coco covered her face with her hands. Then she looked up. "Paige Morgan! You made me look like a dork.

Remember last summer? The sleepover at your house? Your dad said something I won't forget. People who believe in magic are 'nutters.' Now Orion will think I'm a nutter!"

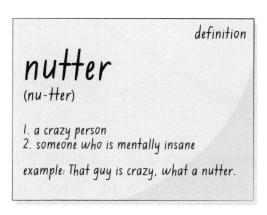

definition

nutter
(nu-tter)

1. a crazy person
2. someone who is mentally insane

example: That guy is crazy, what a nutter.

"You didn't ask him. I did," Paige said. "Let him think I'm the nutter. I don't care. You're the sister I never had. You're my bestie. What harm would it do? None. He can stare at you with those eyes. It can't hurt. And it might help."

"You're my bestie too. Do you really believe he's magical?"

"The world is full of bad stuff. I *want* to believe in this," Paige said. "Why not?"

Coco shook her head. Then she giggled. "Well, I can't believe it. Now my best friend is a nutter. Totally cray-cray."

Paige giggled too.

Lunch was almost over. Kids made their way to class. Paige and Coco followed the stream. The girls saw Orion leave a classroom. He was with Jacob, a nerdy chess player.

Orion had not made many friends. There was Coco and Paige. Jacob, of course. But Orion also liked Joyce. She had autism. Orion connected with her. He called her Joy. The two could talk for hours. Joyce was not chatty with other kids.

Joyce walked down the hall. Flynn was right behind her. He didn't see Orion. Flynn was flapping his arms. He was cawing like a crow. Joyce's hands were moving fast. She seemed to be talking to herself. The school was chaotic as lunch ended.

Suddenly Flynn screamed. He dropped to the floor. "I'm on fire! I'm on fire!" he yelled. "Not again!"

Flynn Morris is the king of DRAMA!

Kids stared at him. Some pointed. Others laughed. Joyce kept walking.

"Dude, chill," a popular boy told him. "There's no fire. You are losing it."

A few kids joked.

"There goes old Flynn again," one said.

Flynn quickly got up and ran.

Paige looked around. Orion's eyes

glowed. No way! She grabbed Coco. "Look!" she hissed. But it was too late.

Orion had turned back to Jacob. It was like nothing had happened.

8
ROCK SOLID

There was a boy named Alex Parsons. He was also singing in the talent contest. He loved pop songs. Everybody said he was great. He sounded like Bruno Mars.

Paige heard kids talking about him. That worried her. What if kids chose the winner? Then Alex would surely win. But the judges were adults. Local high school music teachers would pick the winner. They would choose Coco, for sure. But Coco had to be on point. No goofs. No stage fright.

Paige was with her parents. "The talent show is this Friday," she said.

"Right," her mom said. "You've said so several times. We've had reminders. The family calendar is marked."

"With a Sharpie," her dad added.

SUN	MON	TUES	WED	THU	FRI	SAT
1	2	3	4	5	6	7
8	9	10	11	12	13 TALENT SHOW!	14
15	16	17	18	19	20	21
22	23	24	25	26	27	28
29	30	31				

"You guys are coming, right?" Paige asked.

"Paige?" Dad said. "I wouldn't miss it. What's not to love? Talented kids singing? Sounds great!"

"Of course we're coming," her mom said. "I know you're excited for Coco. I hope she wins. Please, don't be upset if she doesn't. Her voice is lovely. But maybe someone else will be better."

Dad looked over at Paige. "I'm really proud of you," he said. "You are a good friend. Her family has had a hard time. You're always there for her."

"Yes," her mom said. "A lot of girls your age have it easy. They wouldn't want a friend with drama. A friend who couldn't keep up. We're proud of you."

What were her parents saying? Paige

didn't get it. Were they putting down poor people? Was Coco's family drama bad? What did that even mean?

Coco's parents had been through it. They did their best for their kids. But they couldn't afford a lot. Coco wore old clothes. So did her brother and sisters. That didn't make any of them less great.

Paige and Coco were friends. Period. It was not out of charity. This was not some good deed. Coco was a cool person. She was loyal and kind. Did her parents think Coco was beneath her?

"Guys?" Paige said. "Coco is fun. More fun than anyone. I am myself around her. We laugh and share stuff."

"That's nice," Mom said.

"I can talk to her about anything," Paige said. "Sometimes I can't wait to call her.

Even if I just spent all day with her. She is a rock. Solid."

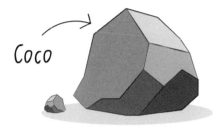

Coco

Her mom stared at her. "You can always talk to us. I hope you know that."

"Of course," her dad said.

"Yeah," Paige said. "I know. And that's great. I love you both. But kids need a best friend too." Paige went to her parents. She gave them each a hug.

Were they jealous? Wow.

9
NERVES

It was the day of the talent show. The show would be at a new high school. It was called Sally Ride High School. The school's theater was big and beautiful.

Everyone was excited. Who would win? But first things first. There was classwork to do.

The hours ticked by. Paige was worried. Coco seemed nervous. She kept moaning. "I can't do it," she said. "The other kids will be so good."

Paige didn't talk about Orion. She hoped he would come. He could work his magic. Would he be there? He didn't promise. But what if he came? Did he have any true power? Paige felt it in her bones. He did!

Flynn had calmed down. He was quieter. The meanness had gone out of him. Nobody thought it would happen. He'd bullied so many kids.

BULLY LIST

☑ Orion
☑ Koral
☑ Jacob
☑ Alex
☑ Joyce

Flynn's bully list

Students felt happier. There weren't as many fights. The lonely kids had paired up. Teachers looked calmer. The principal smiled a lot.

Koral stopped looking over her shoulder. She played more at recess.

A few kids helped Joyce. They walked with her. Some tried to pretend play. They found out Joyce had a great mind. She was super creative.

Showtime! The Morgans drove to the theater. "Does Coco think she'll win? I hope not. She's very talented," Dad said. "But so are the others."

"Everyone's tastes are different," Mom said. "I'm too old for hip-hop. Let's hope the judges are like me. They may like Coco's song."

The Morgans arrived at the theater. Paige saw the Lamars' car. Her parents went ahead. Paige waited. Coco's family walked toward her. Paige hugged them. Then everyone walked inside.

The Morgan family sat near the front. Paige hoped Coco would see her. Seeing a friend would help calm her. Maybe it would be enough.

please!
please!
please!
please!

Would Orion show up? Fingers crossed! But what if he didn't? Was it weird that she'd asked him? She couldn't stop thinking about it.

What had happened to Flynn? It was a happy accident. Orion's stare wasn't magical. The boy wasn't an alien.

Was it all coincidence? All the good stuff? The good feelings? Paige didn't know anymore.

What if Orion came and Coco bombed? He had never promised to come. He'd just smiled. Paige told herself to stop. But she couldn't stop looking. Was Orion here? Nope.

Seats were filling up fast. People were talking and laughing.

10
THE SHOW

Gah! Showtime in 15 minutes. Paige gasped. Orion! He was alone. Wait. Who was he talking to? It was Jacob, his chess club friend. Jacob gave Orion his seat. Orion was in the front row.

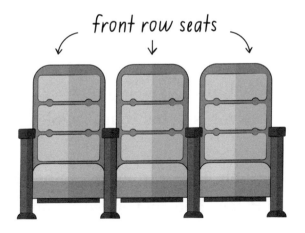

front row seats

The judges took their places. Then the show began. Alex sang a popular rock song. The audience went wild. A girl sang a blues song. Whoa! She sounded like Adele. Another boy sang country. He was good too.

Most kids chose current hits. They were all talented. Just one boy messed up. He forgot the words to his song. People clapped anyway.

And then Coco appeared. She looked lovely. Paige had never seen her more beautiful. She wore a pale yellow dress. It made her honey skin glow. Her hair was soft around her face.

Paige glanced at Orion. She was sitting behind him. The boy looked up. He stared directly at Coco. There was an electric moment. The two seemed to lock eyes.

Coco sang her song. Her powerful voice rose. Every note was clear and perfect. People held their breath.

She nailed it! The theater was quiet. And then the applause came. It crashed down like a tidal wave.

Judging took 10 minutes. Alex won third place. The Adele girl took second.

"First place—it's a big honor," a judge said.

"Everyone is so talented," another judge said.

The third judge took the mic. "The winner is Coco Lamar!" she announced.

winner, winner

chicken dinner

Coco floated to the stage. She hugged the other winners. Someone brought out roses.

"Here's your prize," a judge said. "Use it for college."

Paige clapped wildly. People stood and cheered. There were whistles. Where was Orion? Paige couldn't see the front row.

The house lights came on. Everyone moved toward the exits.

Later both families went out for pizza. Coco was on cloud nine. Her mom shed a few tears. Her dad kept laughing.

Finally the girls had time alone. "You were so calm," Paige said. "How did you do it?"

"Girl," Coco said softly. "I was a wreck. My stomach hurt. I had butterflies—"

stomach full
of butterflies

"Orion," Paige whispered. "That boy! He's got power. Healing power. I don't understand it. How can he do that? Where is he from? I don't know or care."

"I saw him! He looked at me. His eyes lit up. And I felt calm. It was magical," Coco said. "Did you see where he went?"

"No, I lost track," Paige said. "There was too much going on. He seemed to slip away."

"Let's get back to pizza. We'll catch up with him on Monday."

"Deal!" Paige said.

the tastiest pizza ever!

It was Monday. The class was noisy. Kids were talking and laughing. A student passed out papers. Another wrote a math problem on the board.

Ms. Nesbit stood up. "Class," she said.

"I'm sad to tell you this. Orion Wells has moved. I just found out this morning. We'll miss him. Now open your math books. We left off on page 122."

Turn to page 122...

Flynn frowned. Jacob stared out the window. Coco blinked. Paige raised her hand.

"Yes, Paige," Ms. Nesbit said.

"Do you know where he went?" she asked.

"Unfortunately, no. We cannot ask those questions. It's sad when a student moves. He was good for our class. Let's get to our lesson."

Paige raised her hand again.

"Yes," Ms. Nesbit said. "Paige?"

"We should start a kindness club," she said. "In honor of Orion."

"Excellent, Paige," the teacher said. "Yes, we should. Let's talk about it at recess."

Paige had been upset. Orion hadn't even said goodbye. But she'd made peace with it. He'd come into their lives for a reason. His work was done now. Flynn was no longer a bully. Kids weren't mean to each other. Coco had gained self-confidence.

confidence BOOSTED!

The school's kindness club was a hit. Ms. Nesbit was the advisor. Paige was in charge of membership. Coco was president. So many kids wanted to join. Even Flynn.

Paige called it the Orion effect. Was the boy an alien? She didn't think so now. There were no aliens on Earth. Only nutters believed that.

Join the Kindness Club

THE ORION EFFECT

be kind to each other

SIGN UP TODAY!